專門替中國人寫的英文課本

初級本（下冊）

Good morning.

序

李家同

我小的時候，就不怕唸英文，我總覺得物理還有可能使我感到困惑，英文呢？我就搞不清楚英文有什麼難的，只要將生字查一下，就懂得句子的意思了。至於寫英文作文，我也從來不覺得有什麼了不起的，我當然比不上那些洋人，但我很少犯嚴重的文法錯誤。

後來我自己做起國中生的英文義務家教了，我忽然發現一般的國中生認為唸英文是很麻煩的事，英文的生字很多，不容易記，英文文法尤其對一般人不利，動詞的時態常令人頭痛。我總記得，有一次我的學生問我，如何將以下的句子換成被動語氣：

Have you ever read this book?

我完全傻了眼，我花了好多時間才把這個講清楚。

我的女兒在小學裡沒有學過一個英文字，進國中一年級，從A,B,C學起，我想她一定完蛋了，一定會求我幫她的忙，可是她沒有來找我，她和我一樣，有時會被數學或者自然的難題難倒，可是，英文好像從來就不是問題。

我終於想通了，英文對一般中國人是很難的，我對英文沒有問題，絕非我聰明，而是因為我的爸爸媽媽都會講英文，我有什麼問題，問問他們就可以了。我到現在都還記得我的爸爸教我現在完成式是怎麼回事，我的女兒情形相同，她的爸爸媽媽又是會英文的人，有了這種環境，學英文就不難了。

如果家人沒有人會講英文，但有家教來教，或者有財力去進補習班，英文又不難了。

過去，我們國家的小學不教英文，國中英文教科書是國立編譯館編的，我

用這種教科書教當時的國中生，倒還可以應付，學生也勉強可以接受。在我擔任靜宜大學校長的時候，就有一位美國神父常來找我，他一再地說我國的英文教科書太難了，他的理由非常簡單，他說如果美國國中學這麼難的中文，美國的國中生早就造反了。我一直敷衍這位好心的神父，因為我覺得我用那本國立編譯館的英文教科書，還沒有太大的問題。

忽然之間，我的問題來了，我們的教科書不再由國立編譯館編，而是由民間的出版商來編，我教的一位國中一年級學生給我看他的英文教科書，這本書的生字奇難無比，我也去看了一下其他的版本，也都一樣。

從此以後，我就開始好好地想我們國家的英文入門教科書有什麼樣的問題，我想了很久，發現至少**我們的入門教科書有以下幾個缺點：**

1. 我們的英文教科書一律沒有中文說明，連入門的都是如此，也難怪我們的學生覺得學英文好難。試想，假如我們教英國人中文，入門的教科書裡沒有一句英文，試問那些學生如何能懂？

我和一位在大學教英文的教授聊到這點，他也完全同意，他說他想學法文，卻不得其門而入。虧得他運氣好，找到一個網站，這個網站上以英文來解釋法文，他大喜過望，也有了安全感，從此就不再怕法文了。

2. 我們的教科書號稱是包含了英文文法的，但是英文文法談何容易。舉個例子來說，對我們中國人來說，你是、他是、我是、小貓是，任何名詞後面都用同樣的「是」，英文就不同了。I am, You are, He is, They are 等等都不同，這還是現在式，到了過去式，事情就要更加糟了，而且這些文法上的規矩都是沒有道理的，我實在無法告訴學生，為什麼 I 的後面要跟 am，在我看來，全部都用 be，不是很好嗎？

對於初學者而言，he 要用 has，不可以用 have，也是十分麻煩的。

我們的英文教科書，對於這些文法，一概不解釋，因為他們無法解釋，如果他們用中文解釋，乃是犯了大忌，我國的英文教科書裡是不可以用中文的。用英文解釋，那又更不可能，因為小孩子初學英文，如何能看懂英文的解釋

呢？

　　所以我們同學的英文文法基本觀念只好由老師來決定，如果老師教得好，學生就不會犯錯，否則同學就錯誤百出。

　　3. 書中的練習太少了。

　　英文這種東西，是沒有什麼深奧的，只要反覆練習，就一定學得會，一般英文教科書的練習都寥寥可數。學生沒有什麼練習的機會。

　　我實在希望能有一套英文入門教科書，將以上的缺點一一改過來，也就是說，這本書至少應該有以下幾個特色：

　　1. 書中必須有中文翻譯，不僅英文生字有中文解釋，英文句子也要有中文的翻譯，而且也要用中文來解釋。舉例來說，第三人稱，現在式，單數時，動詞要加s，一般的英文教科書並沒有提到，更從不強調，一旦書中有中文解釋，問題就解決了，我們總可以用中文將這個規則說清楚，講明白。

　　2. 書中必須要有中翻英，在過去，中翻英好像是禁忌，那些偉大的學者一再強調，說我們在寫英文句子的時候，必須忘記中文，這種想法，基本假設是我們有一個說英文的環境，大家都只講英文，不講任何其他語言，這樣我們當然就可以用英文的思維方式來寫英文句子。

　　可是，我們沒有這種環境，我們平時都講中文，怎麼可能不從中文想起？中翻英仍然是非常重要的。因為我們都是用中文想的。

　　根據我的經驗，任何一個小孩子，只要他會翻譯一些中文的句子，他就會有好的成就感，大家不要以為「我是一個男孩子」和「他不喜歡我」，這類句子太簡單，其實不然，如果小孩子會出口成章地將這些中文句子正確地譯成英文，他一定會感到十分快樂了。很多初學英文的孩子，會說 "He don't like me."

　　3. 每一課都要非常簡單，舉例來說，否定的句子有兩種，一種是 verb to be 的否定句，另一種是一般動詞的否定，前者可以直接改成否定句，後者必須加一個do動詞，兩者截然不同，入門的教科書應該將這兩種不同的情形分

開來講，讀這本書的人可以循序漸進，慢慢地來，弄懂了一些，再看下一課。

4. 這本書必須不要太貴，所以編排不要太昂貴，越簡單越好，絕對不要有圖畫，更不要有彩色，因為我的心目中有很多家境不太好的孩子，他們根本沒有能力買貴的書。

5. 這本書必須有一個光碟，專門用來訓練發音之用，對於英文初學者，最恐怖的事是不會發音。假如有一個孩子在上課時沒有學會唸一些字，回家又沒有人可以教，他就完全垮掉了。至於學音標，我擔心對初學者是二度傷害，因為英文字母已經很難了，還要認音標，豈不是難上加難？

我現在終於有這兩本入門的書了，文老師寫的書簡單又容易讀，有很多練習，包含中翻英，應該是入門的好書。

我想這兩本書不可能成為學校的正式教科書的，但是這些書卻適合於任何一個初步入門的人，不論老幼。很多老年人，當年沒有學好英文，仍可以用這兩本書作為入門之用。

我在此要給每一位用這本書的老師一個建議：不要趕進度，慢慢來。一再地反覆練習，直到你的學生非常熟悉為止。

我已經用這本書教幾位小朋友了，一開始，我請他們翻譯「我是一個男孩」，他們還結結巴巴說不清楚，過了一陣子，再問他們這種句子，他們會嫌煩，因為他們已經熟得不得了，前些日子，我請他們翻譯「他不是我的老師」，他們也都能順口而出，我高興，他們也高興。昨天，他們會翻譯「他每天上學」這類的句子，而且也會在動詞後面加 S，我正在準備教「他不是每天上學」這種句子。

這兩本書也都有了光碟作伴，如果你不認識書中的字，可以點一下，就會聽到這個字的發音，光碟也有聽寫的功能。希望老師們能夠幫助孩子們利用光碟。

總而言之，我希望很多家中沒有人會講英文的孩子們，以後不會太怕英文，至少這本書裡面都是中文的解釋，應該不至於是天書了。

目次

第十三課 （朗讀光碟 第1軌）

過去式
（肯定句）

過去式用在描寫過去或剛剛發生的事。例如昨天我打了籃球。I played basketball yesterday. 因為是昨天做的事，動詞要用過去式：play→played。

I played basketball yesterday.

13-1　生字

yesterday	昨天
last night	昨晚
last week	上星期
last month	上個月
last year	去年
before	過去，以前
basketball	籃球
walk（walked）	走
find（found）	找到
Japan	日本

I played basketball yesterday.

昨天我打了籃球。

You watched TV last night.

昨晚你看了電視。

She walked to school last week.

上星期她走路上學。

He called his teacher yesterday.

昨天他打了電話給老師。

It found a ball last month.

上個月牠找到了一個球。

You went to Japan last year.

去年你們去了日本。

He read this book before.

以前他讀過這本書。

＊注意 read 的過去式與現在式拼法相同，不過發音不同。

13-3

動詞過去式分為兩種：一種很簡單，只在動詞後加 ed，請看下面的動詞變化：

play → played　玩

call → called　打（電話）

watch → watched　看

（注意：watch 的 ch 發輕音，加 ed 後，ed 唸成 t 的音）

walk → walked　走

（注意：walk 的 k 發輕音，加 ed 後，ed 唸成 t 的音）

like → liked　喜歡

（注意：like 的 k 發輕音，加 ed 後，ed 唸成 t 的音）

  13-4　另一種是不規則動詞變化：

am, is → was（be 動詞）

are → were（be 動詞）

have, has → had　有

eat → ate　吃

go → went　去

read → read　讀

（＊注意：read 過去式的讀法與現在式不同，雖然寫法一樣。）

take → took　拿

find → found　找到

drink → drank　喝

13-5-1 填充

1. I _____（watch）TV last night.

2. I _____（eat）a cake yesterday.

3. She _____（be）a teacher before.

4. He _____（drink）water last night.

5. I _____（call）my mom last night.

6. They _____（eat）cakes last night

7. We _____（play）computer games last week.

8. He _____（take）a shower yesterday.

9. She _____（read）a book last night.

10. He _____（go）home last night.

11. She _____（be）a student before.

12. They _____（listen）to music last night.

13. We _____（eat）breakfast at 7:00A.M.

14. He _____（like）this movie.

15. Your dad _____（like）that book before.

16. Our son _____（eat）lunch at 1:00 A.M.

17. I _____（have）a dog before.

18. My sister _____（have）a cat before.

19. His sisters _____（find）a book.

20. He _____（be）a doctor before.

21. You _____（take）my book yesterday.

22. My daughters _____（play）basketball yesterday.

23. His mom _____（have）this house before.

24. Their brothers and sisters_____（are）in this school before.

25. I _____（read）this book last night.

13-5-2 改錯

1. He walks to school yesterday.

2. My dog find a ball today.

3. I went to school every day.

4. I like to play computer games before.

5. I take a shower last night.

6. I find many books in the house yesterday.

7. She were a teacher before.

8. They was engineers last year.

9. We go to Japan last week.

10. My sister is in this school last year.

11. We are his teachers before.

12. You drink milk last night.

13. I eat a cake yesterday.

14. My son call his teacher last night.

15. His dad is a doctor before.

13-5-3 英文怎麼寫?

1. 我昨晚看了電視。

    _____

2. 你的女兒昨天打電話給你。

    _____

3. 他們的兒子拿了這本書。

    _____

4. 我的媽媽以前打籃球。

    _____

5. 他的爸爸昨晚玩電腦遊戲。

    _____

6. 我找到了這本書。

    _____

7. 他們以前讀過那本書。

    _____

8. 牠昨天找到一隻鳥。

    _____

9. 我們昨天走路上學。

    _____

10. 他們去年去過日本。

    _____

11. 我的女兒以前是一位工程師。

    _____

12. 她的媽媽以前是一位醫生。

    _____

13.　我以前喜歡可樂。

_____

14.　他以前喜歡音樂。

_____

15.　我上星期打了籃球。

_____

第十四課　（朗讀光碟　第 2 軌）

過去式
（be 動詞的否定句和問句）

be 動詞 is 的過去式是 was，be 動詞 are 的過去式是 were。

Were you his teacher before?

14-1 生字

good	好
bad	壞
but	但是
was not → wasn't	be 動詞的過去否定句（用在 I, she, he, it）
were not → weren't	be 動詞的過去否定句（用在 you, they, we）
Mr. → Mister	先生
Ms.	女士

Was she a doctor before?

她以前是醫生嗎？

No, she wasn't. She was an engineer before.

不是。她以前是工程師。

Were they teachers before?

他們以前是老師嗎？

No, they weren't. They were nurses.

不是。他們是護士。

Was he a good singer before?

以前他是個好歌星嗎？

Yes, he was before, but he is a bad singer now.

是，他以前是。但是現在他是個不好的歌星。

Were you Mr. Lin's doctor?

你是林先生的醫生嗎？

No, I wasn't. I was Ms. Chen's doctor.

我不是。我是陳女士的醫生。

14-3　請看 be 動詞過去式「肯定句」的變化表：

以前我是林先生的學生。

I	was	Mr. Lin's	student	before.
You	were	Mr. Lin's	student	before.
He	was	Mr. Lin's	student	before.
She	was	Mr. Lin's	student	before.
We	were	Mr. Lin's	students	before.
You ·	were	Mr. Lin's	students	before.
They	were	Mr. Lin's	students	before.

 14-4　請看 be 動詞過去式「否定句」的變化表：

以前我不是林先生的學生(was 變成 wasn't, were 變成 weren't)

＊注意：第三人稱 he 和 she 要用 wasn't

I	wasn't	Mr. Lin's	student	before.
You	weren't	Mr. Lin's	student	before.
He	wasn't	Mr. Lin's	student	before.
She	wasn't	Mr. Lin's	student	before.
We	weren't	Mr. Lin's	students	before.
You	weren't	Mr. Lin's	students	before.
They	weren't	Mr. Lin's	students	before.

14-5　be 動詞過去式「問句」

和現在式一樣，be 動詞過去式的問句是把 was 和 were 放在句子最前面，請看例句：

Were you his teacher before?你以前是他的老師嗎？

No, I wasn't. 不是，我不是。

I was her teacher. 我是她的老師。

請看下列變化表。

Was	I	Mr. Lin's	student	before?
Were	you	Mr. Lin's	student	before?
Was	he	Mr. Lin's	student	before?
Was	she	Mr. Lin's	student	before?
Were	we	Mr. Lin's	students	before?
Were	you	Mr. Lin's	students	before?
Were	they	Mr. Lin's	students	before?

14-6-1 填填看（用 be 動詞否定句）

1. I _____ their teacher last year.

2. She _____ my doctor before.

3. They _____ at home last month.

4. We _____ your mom's students before.

5. It _____ my dog before.

6. This dog _____ his dog before, but now it is his dog.

7. This book _____ her mother's, but now it is her book.

8. Their sons _____ my students last year.

9. It _____ my computer before.

10. His bird _____ in the house last week.

11. This boy _____ a good singer before.

12. That girl _____ a good student last year.

13. This computer _____ bad last week.

14. His cats _____ big before.

15. I _____ a good student before.

14-6-2 填填看（問句）

1. _____ my dad your teacher before?

    Yes, he _____

2. ＿＿＿＿＿＿＿＿ my daughters your students last year?

　　No, they ＿＿＿＿＿＿＿＿

3. ＿＿＿＿＿＿＿＿ your mother his doctor before?

　　Yes, she ＿＿＿＿＿＿

4. ＿＿＿＿＿＿＿＿ they your teachers last year?

　　No, they ＿＿＿＿＿＿＿

5. ＿＿＿＿＿＿＿＿ their daughter a singer?

　　Yes, she ＿＿＿＿＿＿＿

6. ＿＿＿＿＿＿＿＿ his dog your dog before?

　　No, it ＿＿＿＿＿＿＿＿

7. ＿＿＿＿＿＿＿＿ your mom their teacher last year?

　　Yes, she ＿＿＿＿＿＿＿＿＿＿

8. ＿＿＿＿＿＿＿＿ he an actor before?

　　No, he ＿＿＿＿＿＿＿＿＿＿＿＿

9. ＿＿＿＿＿＿＿＿ she an engineer last year?

　　Yes, she ＿＿＿＿＿＿＿＿

10. ＿＿＿＿＿＿＿＿ you in Japan last month?

　　No, I ＿＿＿＿＿＿＿＿＿

11. ＿＿＿＿＿＿＿＿ he your mom's friend before?

　　Yes, he ＿＿＿＿＿＿＿＿＿

12. ＿＿＿＿＿＿＿＿ his mom and your mom friends before?

　　No, they ＿＿＿＿＿＿＿＿＿ friends.

13. ＿＿＿＿＿＿＿＿ Ms. Lin your dad's teacher before?

　　Yes, she ＿＿＿＿＿＿＿＿

14. ＿＿＿＿＿＿＿＿ his dad your teacher before?

　　No, he ＿＿＿＿＿＿＿

15. _____ your friends in Taichung last week?

No, they _____

14-6-3　英文該怎麼寫？

1. 我以前不是林女士的的學生。

_____

2. 他去年不是我的老師。

_____

3. 我媽媽上星期不在家（at home）。

_____

4. 他爸爸昨天很悲傷（sad）。

_____

5. 這隻狗去年不大。

_____

6. 昨天我不高興（happy）。

_____

7. 我女兒上星期不太高興。

_____

8. 這個女孩去年不是我的朋友。

_____

9. 我上個月不在家。

_____

10. 我的弟弟去年不是工程師。

_____

第十五課 （朗讀光碟 第 3 軌）

過去式

（動詞的否定句和問句）

動詞現在式的否定句是在動詞前加 don't 和 doesn't，過去式的否定句則改用 didn't。不過，不管是第幾人稱 I, you, she, he, it, they, we 過去式否定都用 didn't。問句則是把 Did 放在句首。 例如：Did you go to school yesterday?

Did you do your homework yesterday?

15-1　生字

do, does → did　　　do 和 does 的過去式

did not → didn't　　　過去式否定

listen → listened　　　聽

baseball　　　棒球

America　　　美國

15-2　課文

She listened to music yesterday.	昨天她聽了音樂。
We didn't listen to music yesterday.	昨天我們沒有聽音樂。
Did you listen to music yesterday?	昨天你聽了音樂沒有？
No, I didn't.	昨天我沒有。
He went to America last week.	上星期前他去了美國。
She didn't go to America last week.	上星期前她沒有去美國。
They played baseball last month.	上個月他們打了棒球。
We didn't play baseball last month.	上個月我們沒有打棒球。
Did she play baseball last month?	上個月她打了棒球沒有？
No, she didn't.	她沒有。

＊你還記得嗎？ go 這個動詞很特別，它的過去式是 went。

＊ Did 和 didn't 後面動詞都要用原形。

15-3 請看動詞過去式「肯定句」的變化表：

我昨晚聽了音樂。

I	listened to music	last night.
You	listened to music	last night.
He	listened to music	last night.
She	listened to music	last night.
We	listened to music	last night.
You	listened to music	last night.
They	listened to music	last night.

 15-4 請看動詞過去式「否定句」的變化表：

我昨天沒午睡。

I	didn't	take a nap	yesterday.
You	didn't	take a nap	yesterday.
He	didn't	take a nap	yesterday.
She	didn't	take a nap	yesterday.
We	didn't	take a nap	yesterday.
You	didn't	take a nap	yesterday.
They	didn't	take a nap	yesterday.

15-5　以下是動詞過去式「問句」的變化表：

上個月我吃魚了沒有？

Did I	eat	fish	last month?
Did you	eat	fish	last month?
Did he	eat	fish	last month?
Did she	eat	fish	last month?
Did we	eat	fish	last month?
Did you	eat	fish	last month?
Did they	eat	fish	last month?

15-6-1 填填看

1. Yesterday he went to America, but I _____

   I _____ (go) to Japan. 昨天他去了美國，但是我沒去。我去
   了日本。

2. Last week she played basketball, but he_____

   He _____ (play) baseball.

3. Last month I read this book, but he _____

   He _____ (read) that book.

4. Last night I watched TV, but my mom _____

   She _____(read) books.

5. Yesterday I took a shower, but my friends _____

   They _____ (play) computer games.

6. I went to this school before, but she _____

   She _____ (go) to that school.

7. I liked dogs before, but my dad _____

   He _____ (like) birds.

8. My sister listened to music last night, but I _____

   I _____ (play) baseball.

9. My mom liked that house before, but my dad _____

   He _____ (like) this house.

10. My cat _____（like）fish before, but now it does.

11. His mom _____（drink）milk before, but now she does.

12. Their brothers _____（read）books before, but now they do.

13. Yesterday he _____（go）to Japan. He went to America.

14. I _____（take）his books. I took her books last month.

15. She _____（play）baseball. She played basketball last week.

15-6-2　問答

1. Did you go to school yesterday?

   No, _____. I _____to Taichung.

2. Did they watch TV last night?

   No, _____ They _____ computer games.

3. Did she play baseball last week?

   Yes, _____

4. Did his mom play computer games last night?

   Yes, _____

5. Did his dad play baseball last week?

   No, _____ He _____ basketball.

6. Did she read this book last night?

   Yes, _____

7. Did your dog drink milk yesterday?

   No, _____ It _____ water.

8. Did they go to Japan?

   No, _____ They _____ to America.

9. Did he take a nap yesterday?

Yes, _____

10　Did your teacher play computer games yesterday?

No, _____ He _____ books.

11.　Did his cat eat fish?

Yes, _____

12.　Did you like movies before?

No, _____ I _____ books.

13.　Did you have a cat before?

No, _____ I _____ three dogs.

14.　Did you have a computer last year?

Yes, _____

15.　Did they have dogs before?

Yes, _____

15-6-3　改錯

1.　I didn't went to school yesterday.

2.　She doesn't like that book before.

3.　My mom didn't likes movies before.

4.　My sisters didn't went to America last month.

5.　Did you listened to music last night?

6.　Did she played computer games last night?

7.　My teachers don't like this movie before.

8.　He didn't walks to school last week.

9.　I didn't took a shower last night.

10.　My mom didn't takes a nap yesterday.

11. This doctor didn't reads that book before.
12. My dogs didn't liked fish before.
13. Did your cat likes milk before?
14. Did your dog watched a bird yesterday?
15. Did they watched TV last night?

第十六課　（朗讀光碟　第4軌）

未來式
（肯定句、否定句、問句）

未來式用來表示還沒有發生，但將要發生或以後會發生的事情。未來式很簡單，只要在動詞前加 will 就可以了。另外，不管第幾人稱，I, You, She, He, It, They, We 後面都用 will。

I will be back.

will	將會
later	待會兒
tomorrow	明天
tonight	今晚
next week	下星期
next month	下個月
next year	明年
egg	蛋
come	來
here	這裡

I will read a book later.

我待會兒要讀一本書。

You will take a shower later.

你待會兒要洗澡。

He will go to school next year.

他明年要上學。

She will watch TV tonight.

她今天晚上要看電視。

We will eat eggs tomorrow.

我們明天要吃蛋。

You will play baseball next week.

你們下星期要打棒球。

They will come here next month.

下個月他們會來這裡。

16-3　**請看下表：**

I	will	play basketball	tomorrow.
You	will	listen to music	tonight.
He	will	take a shower	tonight.
She	will	play computer games	later.
It	will	drink water	later.
We	will	go to school	next week.
You	will	call my friend	later.
They	will	eat breakfast	tomorrow.

 16-4

未來式的否定只需在 will 後面加 not，例如：

I will go later.

I will not go later.（I won't go later.）

will not = won't（will not 可以簡寫成 won't）

I	won't	play basketball	tomorrow.
You	won't	listen to music	tonight.
He	won't	take a shower	tonight.
She	won't	play computer games	later.
It	won't	drink water	later.
We	won't	go to school	next week.
You	won't	call my friend	later.
They	won't	eat breakfast	tomorrow.

16-5

未來式問句很簡單，只要把 Will 放在句子前，在句尾再加個問號就可以了。

請看例句：

Will you go to school tomorrow?

Yes, I will.

Will he go to school tomorrow?

（注意：go 用動詞原形）

No, he won't.

Will	you	play basketball	tomorrow?
Will	you	listen to music	tonight?
Will	he	take a shower	tonight?
Will	she	play computer games	tonight?
Will	it	drink water	tonight?
Will	we	go to school	next week?
Will	you	call my friend	tonight?
Will	they	eat breakfast	tomorrow?

16-6-1

下面哪些事情是你明天會做的，請用will，哪些事情是你明天不會做的，請用won't。（這大題沒有標準答案。）

I _____ play computer games tomorrow.

I _____ go to school tomorrow.

I _____ take a nap tomorrow.

I _____ call my friends tomorrow.

I _____ play basketball tomorrow.

I _____ do my homework tomorrow.

I _____ take a shower tomorrow.

I _____ watch TV tomorrow.

I _____ listen to music tomorrow.

I _____ read a book tomorrow.

I _____ play baseball tomorrow.

I _____ eat an egg tomorrow.

I _____ drink Coke tomorrow.

16-6-2 填充

1.　He _____（read）a book tonight.

2.　I _____（listen）to music tomorrow.

3.   She _____（do）her homework later.

4.   We _____ （call）our mom tonight.

5.   They _____ （go）to Japan next month.

6.   We _____ （play）baseball tomorrow.

7.   It _____（eat）an egg later.

8.   You _____ （call）your friend tonight.

9.   I _____ （watch）TV tonight.

10. She _____ （eat）lunch later.

11. My mom and dad _____ （play）cards tonight.

12. Your sister _____ （drink）milk later.

13. My dog _____（drink）water later.

14. His cat _____（eat）fish tonight.

15. Their daughter _____（find）a book later.

16-6-3 問答

1.   Will you go to school tomorrow?

     Yes, _____

2.   Will you watch TV tonight?

     No,_____ I will watch TV tomorrow.

3.   Will you go home today?

     Yes,_____

4.   Will you call your friend tonight?

     No, _____ I will call my friend tomorrow.

5.   Will you play basketball tomorrow?

     Yes,_____

6. Will you eat dinner at 6:00 P.M.?

No, _____ I will eat dinner at 7:00 P.M.

7. Will you do your homework tonight?

Yes,_____

8. Will you take a shower now?

No, _____ I will take a shower later.

9. Will you take a nap now?

Yes,_____

10. Will you drink Coke ?

No, _____I will drink water.

11. Will she go to school tomorrow?

Yes, _____

12. Will this girl play computer games tonight?

No, _____She will play basketball.

13. Will that boy watch TV tomorrow?

Yes, _____

14. Will this cat eat fish tonight?

Yes,_____

15. Will you listen to music tonight?

No, _____ I will watch TV.

16-6-4 英文該怎麼寫？

1. 我明天會去上學。

_____

2. 他下星期會去日本。

_____

3. 你今晚會洗澡嗎？

   _____

4. 我媽媽待會兒要去打棒球。

   _____

5. 我女兒下個月會很高興。

   _____

6. 這個醫生等會兒會讀這本書。

   _____

7. 那位工程師等會兒會睡午覺。

   _____

8. 這個女孩待會兒會打電話給我。

   _____

9. 你的學生今天下午會來嗎？

   _____

10. 他們明天會去打籃球。

    _____

第十七課 （朗讀光碟 第 5 軌）

打招呼

我們剛學完基本的英文文法規則，現在來看看如何把學會的英文靈活運用在生活上。首先我們先學早上、中午或晚上跟家人、朋友、或老師同學見面時，如何用英文來打招呼？

Good morning.

17-1 生字

morning	早上
afternoon	下午
evening	晚上
night	晚上（比 evening 更晚一點）
today	今天
nice	好
dream	夢
too	也

17-2　課文

A：	Good morning.	早安
B：	Good morning.	早安
A：	How are you today?	你今天好嗎？
B：	Fine, thank you.	好，謝謝。
A：	Good-bye.	再見
B：	See you later.	再見
A：	Good afternoon.	午安
B：	Good afternoon.	午安
A：	Good evening.	晚上好
B：	Good evening.	晚上好
A：	Good night.	晚安（睡前）
B：	Good night.	晚安
A：	Have a nice dream.	祝你有個好夢。
B：	You, too.	你也是。

17-3 本課韻文

Good-bye to you.

Good-bye to you.

Good-bye, my dear friend.

I'll see you again.

（用生日快樂 "Happy Birthday to You" 的調子唱）

 17-4 發音練習

good, book, moon, hook, foot, stood, noon, tooth

有時 ou 也發 oo 的音。例如：would 和 should

 17-5 你知道嗎？

打招呼的時候，問你今天好嗎？	How are you today?
如果你覺得今天很好，可以說：	I'm fine. Thank you.
如果覺得還可以，可以說：	I'm O.K.

祝福的話該怎麼說？

Have a nice trip!	祝一路順風！
Have a nice day!	祝你今天愉快！
Have a good time!	祝你玩得愉快！
Have fun!	祝你玩得愉快！

・買完東西後你可以跟店員說："Have a nice day!" 聽到這句祝福的話，一般人一定會接："You, too."

・Good-bye 和 See you later. 的意思一樣，可以交互使用。

介系詞(in, at)

in the morning　　例句：I go to school in the morning.　我上午去上學。
in the afternoon　例句：I take a nap in the afternoon.　我下午睡午覺。
in the evening　　例句：I do my homework in the evening.　我晚上做功課。
at night　　　　　例句：I read books at night.　我晚上讀書。

- "too"(也)的用法：

  I have three brothers.　　　　　我有三個哥哥。
  He has three brothers, too.　　他也有三個哥哥。
  He's a student.　　　　　　　　他是學生。
  I'm a student, too.　　　　　　我也是學生。（或說：Me, too.我也是。）

17-6-1 選選看

1. (   )They took a nap （1）on （2）in （3）at （4）by the afternoon.
2. (   )My dad listens to music （1）on （2）in （3）at （4）by night.
3. (   )My sister takes a shower （1）on （2）in （3）at （4）by the evening.
4. (   )I eat breakfast （1）on （2）in （3）at （4）by the morning.
5. (   )My son takes a shower （1）on （2）in （3）at （4）by the morning.
6. (   )My dog drinks milk （1）on （2）in （3）at （4）by   night.
7. (   )My birds drink water （1）on （2）in （3）at （4）by the afternoon.
8. (   )Their mom plays basketball （1）on （2）in （3）at （4）by   the evening
9. (   )Our daughters play computer games （1）on （2）in （3）at （4）by night.
10. (   )His dad plays soccer （1）on （2）in （3）at （4）by night.

17-6-2 填填看

1. Good _____（早安）
2. Good _____（午安）
3. Good _____ （晚上好）
4. Good _____（晚安）
5. How are you?

    I am _____. Thank you.

6. Good-bye.

   See you _____.

7. I have a dog.

   He has a dog, _____ 他也有一隻狗。

8. I watch TV every day.

   He_____, too.

9. He's reading a book.

   I_____, too.

10. My mom is playing computer games.

    Her mom _____, too.

11. His mom is an engineer.

    My mom _____, too

12. Amy is my teacher.

    She is his teacher, _____

13. He likes eggs.

    I _____, too.

14. She played baseball yesterday.

    I _____, too.

15. He will play basketball later.

    I will _____, too.

第十八課 （朗讀光碟 第6軌）

介紹

日常生活中我們常常要在一些場合介紹自己，或介紹自己的家人或朋友給其他人認識，這些「介紹」用語，英文該怎麼說呢？

18-1　生字

name	名字
Tom	男人名字
Wendy	女人名字
nice	好
meet	遇到
Taiwan	台灣
from	從
uncle	叔叔、伯伯、姨丈、姑丈
aunt	嬸嬸、伯母、阿姨、姑姑

18-2　課文

Tom：	Hi, my name is Tom.	嗨，我的名字叫Tom。
Wendy：	I'm Wendy.	我是 Wendy。
Tom：	Nice to meet you.	幸會。
Wendy：	Nice to meet you, too.	幸會。
Tom：	Where are you from?	你是哪裡人？
Wendy：	I'm from Taiwan.	我是台灣人。
Wendy：	Tom, this is my uncle.	Tom，這位是我的叔叔。
	Uncle John, this is my friend, Tom.	
		叔叔，這是我的朋友，Tom。
Tom：	Nice to meet you.	幸會。
Uncle：	Nice to meet you, too.	幸會。
Wendy：	Tom, this is my aunt.	Tom，這位是我的阿姨。
	Aunt Mary, this is my friend, Tom.	
		阿姨，這位是 Tom。
Tom：	Nice to meet you.	幸會。
Aunt：	Nice to meet you, too.	幸會。

18-3　本課韻文

Where is my friend?

Where is my friend?

Here I am.

Here I am.

How are you today?

Very well. Thank you.

Run and hide.

Run and hide.

（用「兩隻老虎」的調子唱）

 18-4 發音練習

meet, feet, need, teeth, weed, deed, seed, feed

有時 ea 也發 ee 的音。例如：read 和 heat

 18-5　你知道嗎？

- 英文的親戚稱謂沒有我們的複雜，所有的叔叔、伯伯、姑丈、姨丈都叫做 uncle。同樣的，所有的嬸嬸、伯母、姑姑、阿姨、伯母都叫做 aunt。
- 如果有人問你 Where are you from? 你的回答可以是你住的鄉鎮 I'm from Nantou.（南投）。如果在國外，可以回答 I'm from Taiwan.。
- 第一次跟人見面，各自介紹自己的名字 My name is Wendy. 或 I'm John. 之後，對方說：Nice to meet you. 你可以回答：Nice to meet you, too.
- meet 的過去式是 met。

18-6-1 填填看

1. What is your _____?

   My name _____ Tom.

2. What is her name?

   Her _____ is Amy.

3. What is your daughter's name?

   _____name is Amy, too. （用所有格）

4. What are your brothers' names?

   _____names are Tom and John. （用所有格）

5. Nice to meet you.

   _____ to meet you, too.

6. Where are you from?

   I'm _____ Taichung.

7. Where is your pencil?

   _____is on the desk.

8. Where are my books?

   _____ are in the house.

9. Where is my mom?

   _____ is in Taipei.

10. Where are you from?

I am _____ Taiwan.

11. Where _____ your mother from?

_____ is from Taichung.

12. Where is my computer?

_____ is on the desk.

13. Where is his basketball?

_____is on the chair.

14. Where are his cards?

_____ are on the desk.

15. Where is my cake?

It _____ on the chair.

18-6-2　改錯

1. Their son's name are(is) John.

2. My brothers' names is Tom.

3. Where is my pencils?

4. Where is my mom's cakes?

5. Your bicycle is in the house before.

6. I meet my teacher yesterday.

7. Where are my basketball?

8. Where is your brothers?

9. Where are your sister from?

10. She meet my brother last year.

18-6-3 英文該怎麼寫？

1. 他的老師是哪裡人？

   _____

2. 他的老師是美國人。

   _____

3. 你的老師是哪裡人？

   _____

4. 我的老師是日本人。

   _____

5. 他們的老師是哪裡人？

   _____

6. 他們的老師是台灣人。

   _____

7. 我的貓的名字叫 Amy。

   _____

8. 他的狗的名字叫 John。

   _____

9. 我去年遇到 Tom。

   _____

10. 她每天都會遇到 Tom。

    _____

第十九課　（朗讀光碟　第7軌）

你會嗎？

跟朋友聊天時，總會問起對方會不會游泳、踢足球等等，你知道怎樣用英語說嗎？

Can you swim?

sport	運動
of course	當然
can	能、會、可以
can not → cannot → can't	不能、不會、不可以
swim	游泳
soccer	足球

19-2 課文

A： Do you like sports?　　你喜歡運動嗎？

B： Of course!　　當然喜歡！

A： Can you swim?　　你會游泳嗎？

B： Yes, I can. And you?　　我會。你呢？

A： No, I can't.　　我不會。

B： Can you play soccer?　　你會踢足球嗎？

A： Yes, I can.　I can play soccer, but I can't play basketball.
　　我會。我會踢足球，但是不會打籃球。

19-3 請看圖表

◎請問某人會不會某項運動或技能——

Can	you 你	play the piano? 彈鋼琴
Can	it	swim? 游泳
Can	he	play the guitar? 彈吉他
Can	she	play soccer? 踢足球
Can	you 你們	play cards? 玩撲克牌
Can	they	speak English? 說英文

◎ 回答上述問題（會）

Yes,	I can.	I can play the piano.
Yes,	it can.	It can swim.
Yes,	he can.	He can play the guitar.
Yes,	she can.	She can play soccer.
Yes,	we can.	We can play cards.
Yes,	they can.	They can speak English.

◎ 回答上述問題（不會）

No, I can't.	I can't play the piano.
No, it can't.	It can't swim.
No, he can't.	He can't play the guitar.
No, she can't.	She can't play soccer.
No, we can't.	We can't play cards.
No, they can't.	They can't speak English.

19-5　本課韻文

Dear Jim,

Can you swim?

Can you sing the ABCs?

Yes, I can.

Yes, I can.

I can swim and sing the ABCs.

Dear Don,

Can you swim?

Can you sing the ABCs?

No, I can't.

No, I can't.

I can't swim and sing the ABCs.

 19-6　發音練習

swim, slip, hit, fix, fit, zip, bit, kick

請注意以下兩組發音的不同：

slip, sleep

fit, feet

hit, heat

19-7　你知道嗎？

• Can 後面必須接動詞，而且一定要是原形動詞喔！

例如：I can play the piano. play是原形動詞，不需要加s(plays),也不需要變

成過去式（played）。

can 和 can't 的意思是「會」，「不會」；另一個意思是「能」，「不能」。

例如：

> I can't drink coffee.（我不能喝咖啡。）
>
> I can't meet you now.（我現在不能見你。）
>
> I can't watch TV now.（我現在不能看電視。）

- soccer 是英式足球，世界杯足球賽就是 soccer。 football 是美式足球。
- 英文裡有些名詞有單數和複數之分，複數要加 s。 sport 是一種運動。 sports 是很多種運動。

19-8-1 填填看

1. Can you swim?

   Yes, I _____. I can swim.

2. Can she swim?

   No, she_____. She can't swim.

3. Can you play baseball?

   No, I _____. I can't play baseball.

4. Can she _____ computer games?

   Yes, she _____. She can play computer games.

5. Can they play basketball?

   Yes, they_____. They can play basketball.

6. Can your dad play baseball?

   No, he _____. He can't play baseball.

7. Can your mom swim?

   Yes, she _____. She _____swimming now.

8. Can your sister play soccer?

   No, she _____, but she _____ play basketball.

9. Can you walk to school?

   No, I _____. I can't walk to school.

10. Can she play the piano?

No, she _____, but she _____play the guitar.

11.   Can they play the guitar?

Yes, they _____. They _____ play the piano, too.

12.   Can you play soccer?

No, I _____, but I _____ play baseball.

13.   Can your son play the guitar?

No, he _____, but he _____play the piano.

14.   Can his daughter play the piano?

Yes, she _____. She_____play the guitar, too.

15.   Can you read this book?

Yes, I _____. It's a good book.

19-8-2 改錯

1.   She can walks（walk）to school.

2.   Can your dog drank milk?

3.   It can't drinks milk.

4.   My mom can swims.

5.   Her sister can't played baseball.

6.   His mom can plays soccer.

7.   Their dad can plays cards.

8.   His daughter can played computer games.

9.   She can't reads this book.

10.   Can he plays soccer?

11.   She can't reads this book.

12.   My mom can't swims.

13. He can't met you now.
14. You can't listened to music now.
15. I can't found my dog.

19-8-3 英文該如何寫？

1. 我不會彈鋼琴。

   _____

2. 我的哥哥不會游泳。

   _____

3. 他的妹妹不會踢足球。

   _____

4. 她媽媽不會說英文。

   _____

5. 我們的爸爸不會彈吉他。

   _____

6. 我今天不能跟你見面。

   _____

7. 他明天不能去學校。（tomorrow）

   _____

8. 我現在不能喝牛奶。

   _____

9. 他們現在不能回家。（go home）

   _____

10. 我今天不能洗澡。

   _____

第二十課　（朗讀光碟 第8軌）

星期幾？

有時候會弄不清楚今天是星期幾，該怎麼用英文問外國人呢？有時候想知道別人星期幾要做什麼，又該怎麼問呢？

20-1　生字

day	天
today	今天
weekend	週末
comic books	漫畫書
about	關於(介系詞)
Sunday =Sun.	星期日
Monday= Mon.	星期一
Tuesday= Tue.	星期二
Wednesday= Wed.	星期三
Thursday=Thu.	星期四
Friday=Fri.	星期五
Saturday=Sat.	星期六

20-2 課文

A： What day is today?　　　今天星期幾？

B： It's Sunday.　　　今天是星期天。

A： What do you do on Saturday and Sunday?

　　　　　　　你星期六和星期天做什麼？

B： I watch TV and play computer games on weekends.
　　 How about you?

　　 週末我看電視和玩電腦遊戲。你呢？

A： I read comic books.　　我看漫畫書。

B： What do you do on Monday, Tuesday, Wednesday,
　　 Thursday, and Friday?

　　 你星期一、星期二、星期三、星期四、和星期五做什麼？

A： I go to school.　　　我去上學。

＊一星期七天每個都有簡稱，就是全名的前三個字母，例如星期日全
名為 Sunday，簡稱取前三個字母：Sun.記得要加縮寫符號(.)喔！

20-3

上星期、這星期、下星期該怎麼說？

上星期幾	這星期幾	下星期幾
last Sunday	this Sunday	next Sunday
last Monday	this Monday	next Monday
last Tuesday	this Tuesday	next Tuesday
last Wednesday	this Wednesday	next Wednesday
last Thursday	this Thursday	next Thursday
last Friday	this Friday	next Friday
last Saturday	this Saturday	next Saturday

 20-4　本課韻文

Sunday, Monday, Tuesday, and Wednesday,

Thursday, Friday, and Saturday.

Seven days, seven days,

There are seven days,

In a week, in a week.

 20-5　發音練習

bay, may, day, play, say, way, pay, lay, ray, hay

20-6 你知道嗎？

- 英文中的名詞有「可數」與「不可數」之分，可數的名詞有 book, cat, dog, girl, boy, daughter, son, brother, sister等等。可數的名詞超過一個要加s，如：two books, three cats, four dogs。不可數的名詞不能加s，如：water, milk, coffee(咖啡), tea(茶)等等。不過這些不可數的名詞如果加上單位後就可以數了。如：two cups of tea(兩杯茶)，three cups of coffee(三杯咖啡)。

- 星期幾前面的介系詞用 on ，例如：

  I don't go to school on Saturday and Sunday.

  I watch TV on Saturday.

  I play basketball on Monday.

20-6-1 選選看

1. (　　) I usually take a shower（1)at（2)in（3)by（4)on 5:00 P.M.

2. (　　) I can't meet you（1)at（2)in（3)by（4)on the evening.

3. (　　) She can't play（1)at（2)in（3)by（4)on night.

4. (　　) My mom will meet you（1)at（2)in（3)by（4)on Sunday.

5. (　　) Her brother goes to school（1)at（2)in（3)by（4)on bus.

6. (　　) I found a dog（1)at（2)in（3)by（4)on the afternoon.

7. (　　) They will meet the singer（1)at（2)in（3)by（4)on the evening

8. (　　) Who will come（1)at（2)in（3)by（4)on night?

9. (　　) What do you usually do（1)at（2)in（3)by（4)on 12:00 P.M.?

10. (　　) His son usually plays the guitar（1)at（2)in（3)by（4)on Friday.

20-6-2 填填看

1.　　What ＿＿＿＿＿ is today? It's Sunday.

　　　你會拼寫出下面星期幾的全名嗎？

2.　　Sun. = ＿＿＿＿＿＿

3.　　Mon. = ＿＿＿＿＿＿

4.　　Tue. = ＿＿＿＿＿＿

5.　　Wed. = ＿＿＿＿＿＿

6.　　Thu. = ＿＿＿＿＿＿

7.   Fri. =   _____

8.   Sat. =   _____

9.   What do you do on Monday?

     I _____ to school.

10. When do you watch TV?

     I watch TV on _____（週末）＊某一個週末：a weekend, 所

     有的週末：weekends

11. When does your daughter play computer games?

     She _____ computer games on _____（星期三）

12. When do they play soccer?

     They play soccer _____ Thursday.

13. What day is today?

     It's _____（星期六）

14. What day is your birthday（生日）?

     My birthday is _____ Wednesday.

15. What did you do on your birthday?

     I _____ a cake.（吃蛋糕）

16. What will you do next Saturday?

     I _____ do my homework.

17. What did you do last Friday?

     I _____the piano.

18. What will you do this Thursday?

     I _____ watch TV.

19. Did you meet your teacher this Wednesday?

     Yes, I did. I _____ my teacher in the school.

20. Did you do your homework last Tuesday?

No, I _____.

20-6-3 英文該怎麼寫？

1. 我星期天都在家看電視。
   I watch TV at home on Sunday.

2. 他的姐姐星期一都去學校。

   _____

3. 我星期四都不彈鋼琴。

   _____

4. 我星期三都在家睡午覺。

   _____

5. 他的狗星期五都睡午覺。

   _____

6. 他們的媽媽星期六都打籃球。

   _____

7. 上星期五我跟我的醫生見了面。

   _____

8. 下星期二我會去踢足球。

   _____

9. 這星期一我會去見我的老師。

   _____

10. 下星期六我會去美國(America)。

    _____

第二十一課 （朗讀光碟 第9軌）

購物

上街買東西時看到喜歡的東西，我們要怎麼問價錢呢？如果我們覺得東西的價錢合宜，想要買下來的話，又該怎麼說呢？

How much is it?

恐龍展

21-1 生字

help	幫忙
look for	尋找
would like	想要……
shirt	襯衫
blue	藍色
size	尺寸
small	小
how much	多少
hundred	百
NT dollar	台幣

A 是店員，B 是顧客

A： Hi, may I help you?　　　　　　嗨，我可以幫你忙嗎？

B： I'm looking for a shirt.　　　　　我在找件襯衫。

A： What color would you like?　　　你想要什麼顏色？

B： I would like blue.　　　　　　　我想要藍色。

A： What is your size?　　　　　　　你的尺寸是多少？

B： Size small.　　　　　　　　　　小號尺寸。

A： Here you are.　　　　　　　　　在這裡。

B： How much is it?　　　　　　　　多少錢？

A： It's two hundred NT dollars.　　　台幣 200 元。

21-3　本課歌曲

Red, red, red, touch your head.

Blue, blue, blue, tie your shoes.

Brown, brown, brown, touch the ground.

White, white, white, take a bite.

Black, black, black, touch your back.

Purple, purple, purple, draw a circle.

Pink, pink, pink, give a wink.

Gray, gray, gray, shout hurray!

 21-4　發音練習

shirt, bird, dirty, sir, skirt

blur, fur, hurt, church

clerk, her

21-5　你知道嗎？

• 一般商店裡的衣服通常分為四種尺寸：超大號（extra large=XL）、大號（large=L）、中號（medium=M）、小號（small=S）。

• 如果有人問你要杯水來喝：May I have a glass of water?你把玻璃杯遞給他時可以說：Here you are.或是說：There you are.

　請看下列例句：

May I have this book?

Yes. Here you are.

May I have that pencil?

Yes. There you are.

• 如果想要什麼東西時可以用 would like 來表達：What would you like, tea or
  coffee?

I would like coffee.

• look for 尋找；be looking for 正在尋找

What are you doing?　你在做什麼？

I 'm looking for my cat.　我正在找我的貓。

• How much 多少

How much money do you have?

I have nine hundred NT dollars.（我有900元台幣）

如果你有900美金可以說 I have nine hundred dollars.

• What color does he like?	他喜歡什麼顏色？
He likes yellow.	他喜歡黃色。
What color does she like?	她喜歡什麼顏色？
She likes green.	她喜歡綠色。
What color do they like?	他們喜歡什麼顏色？
They like black.	他們喜歡黑色。
What color do you like?	你喜歡什麼顏色？
I like white.	我喜歡白色。
What color do you like?	你喜歡什麼顏色？
I like _____.	我喜歡_____

・代名詞：我們有時會用 she, he, it, they 代替名詞，例如：

How much is that shirt?

我們用 it 代替 shirt：

It is 300NT dollars.

How much are your books?

我們用 they 代替 books：

They are 500NT dollars.

21-6 練習題

21-6-1 填填看

1.   How much is the dog?

     _____ eight hundred NT dollars.

2.   How much is that pencil?

     _____ five NT dollars.

3.   How much are your books?

     _____ three hundred NT dollars.

4.   How much are your chair and desk?

     _____ five hundred NT dollars.

5.   How much is your brother's shirt?

     _____ two hundred NT dollars.

6.   What color is your shirt?

     It's _____ （黃色）

7.   What color is your dog?

     It's _____ （白色）

8.   What color does your mom like?

     She _____ brown. （棕色）

9.   What color does your brother like?

     He _____ black. （黑色）

10. What are you looking for?

I'm looking for a _____（電腦）

11. What is he looking for?

He's looking for a black _____（襯衫）

12. What is your daughter looking for?

She's looking for a _____（小鳥）

13. What are your friends looking for?

They're looking for a _____ _____（好書）

14. What is your cat looking for?

It's looking for _____（牛奶）

15. What are they looking for?

They're looking for _____ son.（他們的兒子）

21-6-2　英文該怎麼寫？

1. 我在找一本小書。

   _____

2. 我的姊姊在找一台好的電腦。

   _____

3. 他的鳥在找水。

   _____

4. 我們的老師在找一枝鉛筆。

   _____

5. 她在找她的媽媽。

   _____

6. 這隻鳥在找一個蛋。

   _____

7.   他們女兒在找一隻紫色的鳥。（purple）

_____

8.   我在找一件紅襯衫。（red）

_____

9.   這位醫生在找她的筆。

_____

10.   他們的狗在找牠的媽媽。

_____

21-6-3 改錯

1.   How much is（are）your houses?（你這些房子值多少錢？）
2.   How much are their cat?
3.   I doesn't like this color.
4.   My sisters doesn't like black cats.
5.   What color do he like?
6.   His father don't have money.
7.   Our mom don't watch TV.
8.   She like this computer.
9.   What are his size?
10.   She can't watches TV tonight.
11.   I meet my students last Friday.
12.   I walk to school last Monday.
13.   She will plays computer games this Saturday.
14.   My sister will reads this book tonight.
15.   My brother reads that book last Wednesday.

第二十二課 （朗讀光碟 第 10 軌）

比較

日常生活中，我們常需要比較東西的大小、人的高矮，有時需要說某樣東西比較好，這些英文都該怎麼說呢？

You are shorter than I am.

22-1 生字

big	大
even	甚至
bigger	更大
bag	袋子
so	這麼的
small	小
smaller	更小
tall	高
taller	更高
than	比較
short	矮，短
worry	擔心
shorter	更矮，更短

A： Wow, this dog is big!　　　哇！這隻狗好大！

B： Look, that dog is even bigger.　看！那隻狗甚至更大！

A： This bag is so small.　　　這個袋子這麼小。

B： That bag is smaller.　　　那個袋子更小。

A： You are tall.　　　　　你好高噢！

B： Look, she is taller than I am.　看！她比我更高！

A： I'm short.　　　　　　我好矮。

B： Don't worry, I'm shorter than you are.

　　　　　　　　　　別擔心，我比你還矮。

22-3 本課韻文

Don't worry, I'm shorter than you are.
Don't worry, I'm older than you are.
Don't worry, I'm smaller than you are.
Don't worry, I'm slower than you are.

 22-4 發音練習

bigger, finger, slipper, player, teacher, winner, hotter, smaller

 22-5 你知道嗎？

old→ older than   young→younger than

He is older than I am. 他比我年紀大（現在都說成：He is older than me.）
I am younger than he is. 我比他年紀小。（現在都說成：I am younger than him.）

其他比較級和最高級的形容詞：
big→ bigger than   small→smaller than
（大→較大）   （小→較小）
long→longer than   short→shorter than
（長→較長）   （短→較短）
＊good→ better than ＊bad→ worse than
（好→較好）   （差→較差）
light→lighter than   ＊heavy→heavier than
（輕→較輕）   （重→較重）
clean→cleaner than   ＊dirty→ dirtier than

（乾淨→較乾淨）　　　　（髒→較髒）

old→older than　　　　new→newer than

（舊→較舊）　　　　　（新→較新）

fast→faster than　　　slow→slower than

（快→較快）　　　　　（慢→較慢）

- 一般形容詞的比較級加 er 即可，但也有例外的情形。本課介紹的 good, better 和 bad, worse 就是一個很特別的例子，除了死背，別無他法。另外，big 裡的 i 是短母音，後面緊接著的子音 g 要重複一次，寫為 bigger。heavy 和 dirty 加 er 時，後面的 y 要改為 i，因此，比較級變為 heavier 和 dirtier。

 22-5-1　so 後面加形容詞，有加強語氣的作用。如：

so beautiful(這麼美)：She's so beautiful.

so sweet(這麼甜)：This cake is so sweet.

so cheap(這麼便宜)：This bag is so cheap.

so expensive (這麼貴)：This shirt is so expensive.

 22-5-2

Don't worry 叫人別擔心。Don't 後面加一個動詞，都是叫人不要做某件事情。例如：

Don't talk.	別說話	Don't sleep.	別睡覺
Don't go to school.	別上學	Don't take a shower.	別洗澡
Don't watch TV.	別看電視	Don't play computer games.	

別玩電腦遊戲

22-6   練習題

22-6-1 填填看

1. John is old, but Mary is _____（比較老）

2. This house is big, but that house is _____（比較大）

3. This room is clean, but that room is _____（比較乾淨）

4. Amy's car is too small. She wants a _____car.（比較大的）

5. This dog is young, but that dog is _____（比較年輕）

6. This chair is high, but that chair is _____（更高）

7. This book is good, but that one is _____.（比較好）

8. She's slow, but her sister is _____.（更慢的）

9. This book is bad, but that book is _____.（比較差）

10. This desk is heavy, that box is _____.（更重）

11. I'm _____ than he is.（old）

12. She's _____than I am.（short）

13. They're _____than we are.（tall）

14. This book is _____ than that book.（heavy）

15. They're _____than she is.（young）

16. We're _____than they are.（fast）

17. He's _____than his sister.（slow）

18. Her mom is _____than her dad.（tall）

19. This house is _____ than that house.（clean）

20.　This cat is _____ than that cat.（dirty）

22-6-2　英文該怎麼寫？

1.　我比我哥哥高。

_____

2.　他比我弟弟矮。

_____

3.　我媽媽（年紀）比我爸爸大。

_____

4.　我妹妹比我慢。

_____

5.　這隻貓比那隻貓快。

_____

6.　這本書比那本書好。

_____

7.　我的弟弟比我重。

_____

8.　他們比我們快樂。

_____

9.　這隻鳥比那隻鳥小。

_____

10.　這部電影比那部電影長。

_____

11.　這張書桌比那張椅子輕。

_____

12.　今晚別看電視。

_____

13.　星期一別打籃球。

_____

14.　星期三別彈鋼琴。

_____

15.　星期四別睡午覺。

_____

第二十三課 （朗讀光碟 第11軌）

表示喜歡或不喜歡

日常生活中，我們常需要表達自己的好惡，有時我們也要問別人對某件事情的看法，這些英文都該怎麼說呢？

How do you like this white dog?

23-1 生字

very much	很
cute	可愛
too	也，太
movie	電影
not at all	一點也不
boring	無聊
O.K.	普通，不好不壞，還可以

23-2 課文

A： How do you like this white cat?

你覺得這隻白貓如何？

B： It's very cute. I like it very much.

牠很可愛。我很喜歡牠。

A： Do you like this cat or that cat?

你喜歡這隻貓還是那隻貓？

B： I like this one better.

我比較喜歡這一隻。

A： How do you like this movie?

你喜歡這部電影嗎？

B： I don't like it at all. It's too boring.

我一點都不喜歡。它太無聊了。

A： Did you like that movie?

你喜歡那部電影嗎？

B： It was O.K.

還可以。

23-3 本課韻文

I like this music.
I like it very much.
I don't like that music.
I don't like it at all!

I like this singer.
I like her very much.
I don't like that singer.
I don't like him at all!

 23-4 發音練習

like, bike, pipe, Mike, bite, nice, hike, kite
high, fight, tight, might
pie, tie
fly, buy

 23-5 你知道嗎？

受格
I → me
you → you
he → him
she → her
it → it

we → us

they → them

you → you

例如：

How do you like Amy? （你喜歡Amy嗎？）

I like her very much. She's a nice person. （我很喜歡她。她是個好人。）

How do you like your teachers? （你喜歡你的老師嗎？）

I like them very much. They are good teachers. （我喜歡他們。他們是好老師。）

How do you like this computer game? （你喜歡這個電腦遊戲嗎？）

I don't like it at all. It's boring. （我一點也不喜歡。它很無聊。）

How do you like your English class? （你喜歡你的英文課嗎？）

I like it very much. It's not boring at all. （我喜歡。它一點也不無聊。）

 23-5-1 "too"（也，太）的兩種用法：

I like my English teacher.

My sister likes her, too. （也）

How do you like this book?

It's too boring. I don't like it at all. （太）

・如果你有一個綠色的手提袋，你可以說：I have a green bag.，你的朋友也正好有一個綠色的手提袋，他可以說：I have a green bag, too.。
　如果你不喜歡可樂I don't like Coke.，你的朋友也正好不喜歡可樂，這時他可以說：I don't like Coke, either.。

too 和 either 意思都是「也」，不過，too 用在肯定句；either 用在否定句。

 23-5-2

like 的後面也可以接動詞原形，表示喜歡做某個動作，例如：

I like to read books.

I like to play computer games.

I like to watch TV.

I like to listen to music.

＊注意：兩個動詞中間一定要加 to

　　例如：like 和 read ，like 和 play ，like 和 watch ，like 和 listen 中間一定要
　　加 to 。

23-6-1 填填看

1. How do you like my house?

   I like _____ very much. It's so big.

2. How do you like my new shirts?（新襯衫）

   I like _____ very much. They have nice colors.（顏色很好看）

3. How do you like this music?

   I like_____ very much. It's good.

4. Does he like this computer game?

   No, he doesn't like _____ at all.

5. Does she like that purple shirt？

   She _____ it very much. It has a nice color.

6. I like eggs.

   She likes _____, too.

7. I like to drink Coke.

   My brother _____ it, too.

8. My dad likes this computer game.

   His dad likes _____, too.

9. I like your new shirts.

   My mom likes _____, too.

10. She likes her new bicycle.（簡稱為bike）

We like _____, too.

11. How do you like his new bike?

It's very nice. We _____ it very much.

12. How do you like this yellow cat?

It's so _____（可愛）

13. Do you like English?

No, I don't. It's so _____（無聊）

14. Do you like this English book?

Yes, I do. I like _____ very much.

15. Does your dad like to watch TV?

No, _____ doesn't.

16. Do your friends like to speak English?

Yes, _____ do.

17. Does her mom like to play the guitar?

No, not at _____

18. Do your teachers like to eat fish?

Yes, _____ do.

19. Does his cat like to eat fish, too?

No, not _____ all.

20. Do you like to drink coffee?

Yes, I do. I like _____ very much.

23-6-2 改錯

1. I like watch TV.

2. He like to take a shower.

3.　My sister likes read English books.

4.　His brother don't like to eat fish.

5.　This doctor likes play computer games.

6.　Your cats are cute. I like it very much.

7.　Do you like your teacher? Yes, I do. I like he very much.

8.　I don't like go to school.

9.　He don't like to play soccer.

10.　My friend don't like to play the guitar.(彈吉他)

11.　I don't like go to school today.

12.　He don't like to eat eggs.

13.　My cats like watch birds.

14.　He don't like fish at all.

15.　We don't like play basketball at all.

23-6-3　用英文怎麼寫？

1.　我喜歡每天洗澡。

_____

2.　他一點也不喜歡看電視。

_____

3.　這本英文書真無聊。

_____

4.　我的媽媽不喜歡吃魚。

_____

5.　我的弟弟也不喜歡吃魚。(either)

_____

6.　　他喜歡打棒球嗎？

    _____

7.　　我的老師很喜歡彈吉他。

    _____

8.　　她不喜歡喝牛奶。

    _____

9.　　我的爸爸不喜歡紫色的襯衫。（shirts）

    _____

10.　　她的女兒不喜歡黑色的袋子。（bags）

    _____

第二十四課 （朗讀光碟 第 12 軌）

形容長相

round	圓的
face	臉
eye	眼睛
hair	頭髮
sure	確定
hand	手

24-2　課文

A：　What does he look like?

他長得像什麼樣子？

B：　He has a round face and two big round eyes.

他有一張圓臉和兩個大圓眼睛。

A：　Is he very tall?

他很高嗎？

B：　Yes, he is taller than I am.

對，他比我高。

A：　Does he have long hair?

他有沒有留長髮？

B：　I'm not sure.

我不確定。

A：　Does he have big hands?

他有沒有一雙大手？

B：　His hands are smaller than my hands.

他的手比我的手小。

24-3　本課韻文（用「倫敦鐵橋」曲調）

Head, shoulders, knees, and toes, knees and toes.（重複兩次）

Eyes and ears and mouth and nose,

Head shoulders knees and toes, knees and toes.

 韻文中有關身體部分的生字

head	頭
shoulder	肩膀
knee	膝蓋
toe	腳趾頭
eye	眼睛
ear	耳朵
mouth	嘴巴
nose	鼻子

 24-4　發音練習

head, bed, pet, bet, net, neck, fed, met, deck, get, wet

24-5　你知道嗎？

・人有一對眼睛、一對耳朵、兩個肩膀、兩隻手、兩個膝蓋，十個腳趾，所以在本課韻文裡eyes, ears, shoulders, hands, knees, toes都要用複數，要加 s。

・like 這個字有兩種意思，一個是「喜歡」，我們上節課有教過：I like birds.；另一個意思是「像」：He is like my brother.（他像我的哥哥）。注

意前面要加 be 動詞。

＊注意：like 和 be like 這兩個用法不要混用。

- hair 頭髮，屬於不可數的名詞，所以不能加 s。其他不可數的名詞還有 milk, coffee, water, tea。可數的名詞有 eyes, hands, brothers, sisters, girls, boys。

24-6-1 填填看

1.   He has long hair. I have _____ hair.（短頭髮）

2.   Her hands are big. My hands are _____.（小）

3.   My mother's head is _____（big）than my head.

4.   His legs are _____（long）than my legs.

5.   What does she look like?

      She has long _____（長腿）

6.   What does your cat look like?

      It has small _____（小眼睛）

7.   What does your teacher look like?

      He is very _____（很矮）

8.   What does your brother look like?

      He has a big _____（大頭）

9.   What does that actor look like?

      He has a big _____（大鼻子）

10.   What do they look like?

      They have big _____（大耳朵）

11.   What does your cat look like?

      It has four yellow _____（四條黃腿）

12.   What does your dog look like?

It has a big _____(一張大嘴巴)

13. What is it on your _____?(你肩膀上的是什麼？)

It's a bird.

14. What is it on your _____?(你頭上是什麼？)

It's a hat. (一項帽子。)

15. What is it in your _____?(你袋子裡面是什麼？)

It's a book.

16. Where _____ your hands?

They're here.

17. Where _____your mouth?

It's here.

18. Where _____ your nose?

It's here.

19. Where _____ your knees?

They're here.

20. Where _____ your toes?

They're here.

24-6-2　英文該怎麼寫？

1. 看，那隻怪獸(monster)有兩個頭！

_____

2. 看，這隻怪獸有五隻手！

_____

3. 看，這隻怪獸有七個嘴巴！

_____

4.　看，這隻狗有五條腿。

＿＿＿＿＿＿＿＿＿＿＿＿＿＿＿＿＿＿＿＿＿＿＿

5.　看，這隻貓有三個耳朵！

＿＿＿＿＿＿＿＿＿＿＿＿＿＿＿＿＿＿＿＿＿＿＿

6.　你的鼻子在哪裡？

＿＿＿＿＿＿＿＿＿＿＿＿＿＿＿＿＿＿＿＿＿＿＿

7.　你的手在哪裡？

＿＿＿＿＿＿＿＿＿＿＿＿＿＿＿＿＿＿＿＿＿＿＿

8.　你的耳朵在哪裡？

＿＿＿＿＿＿＿＿＿＿＿＿＿＿＿＿＿＿＿＿＿＿＿

9.　你的腳趾頭在哪裡？

＿＿＿＿＿＿＿＿＿＿＿＿＿＿＿＿＿＿＿＿＿＿＿

10.　你的肩膀在哪裡？

＿＿＿＿＿＿＿＿＿＿＿＿＿＿＿＿＿＿＿＿＿＿＿

下冊總複習

I. 選擇題

1. (　) He (1) was (2) is (3) did my teacher before.
2. (　) They (1) meet (2) met (3) will meet that girl next Tuesday.
3. (　) His mom and dad (1) is go (2) will go (3) went to Japan next week.
4. (　) This engineer (1) finded (2) finds (3) found a dog last Saturday.
5. (　) Their sister (1) taked (2) took (3) is taking a shower yesterday.
6. (　) How much (1) is (2) does (3) are this table?
7. (　) (1) Does (2) Will (3) Did he go to America last month?
8. (　) Her nurse (1) can't (2) don't (3) isn't read English books.
9. (　) Is your house (1) biger (2) big (3) bigger than his house?
10. (　) My daughter (1) drinks (2) drank (2) drinked coffee this afternoon.
11. (　) Will her student (1) come (2) came (3) comes here tonight?
12. (　) My brother is taller than (1) I (2) I do (3) I am.
13. (　) My uncle (1) calls (2) called (3) calling my mom last night.
14. (　) She likes (1) to drink (2) drink (3) drinks tea.
15. (　) Their dog (1) weren't (2) won't (3) wasn't at home last week.
16. (　) Our son (1) won't (2) don't (3) isn't take a nap this afternoon.
17. (　) He (1) isn't (2) wasn't (3) will be my mom's student before.
18. (　) My doctor can (1) plays (2) played (3) play the piano.
19. (　) This engineer likes (1) read (2) reads (3) to read books.
20. (　) (1) Can (2) Is (3) Does their sister find a good book next week?

II . 填充題

1. He _____ play the piano, but he can play the guitar.

2. My sister _____ go to Japan tomorrow.（不會去）

3. His mom is an _____, my mom is an engineer, too.

4. I can't play the piano, he can't play the piano, _____.（也不會）

5. How much _____ your guitar?

6. She _____ do her homework last Saturday.（沒有做功課）

7. My mom _____ play the guitar last Friday.（沒有彈吉他）

8. _____ you call your teacher next Thursday?

9. My sister _____ a cake on her birthday.（吃了）

10. My aunt is _____ than my uncle.（年紀比較大）

11. My uncle _____ meet my teacher next Monday.（不能見）

12. _____ you her student before?

13. _____ you read this English book last week?

14. _____ he play the guitar next Tuesday?

15. My friends' _____ are Amy, John, and Tom.（名字）

16. She doesn't like to _____ to music.

17. He _____(find) a dog in Uncle John's house last Friday.

18. This book is _____（更差）than that book.

19. What is it_____ your shoulder? It's a bird.（肩膀上）

20. My aunt is _____ America.（美國人）

III . 問答

1. Where is your uncle from?

   _____（Nantou 南投）

2. Can you swim?

Yes, _____

3. What would you like?

I would like _____（一件紫色的襯衫）

4. Did you find a good book in your teacher's house yesterday?

No, _____

5. Were you his student before?

Yes, _____

6. What did your mom do before?

She was _____（一位老師）

7. Who did she call last night?

She _____（她的朋友）

8. Did your daughter play computer games last Tuesday?

No, _____

9. Did you read books or listen to music last night?

I _____（聽音樂）

10. When will he do his homework?

He _____（待會兒 later）

11. Will Amy be your English teacher next year?

Yes, _____

12. Which dog is older?

My_____

13. What color is your bag?

It's _____（棕色）

14. What will you do on this weekend?

I _____（彈鋼琴）

15.   How do you like this computer game?

It's_____（無聊）

16.   How much is your yellow bag?

It's_____（100 元台幣）

17.   What are you looking for?

I_____（一件乾淨的 clean 襯衫）

18.   What is your aunt's name?

Her _____（Amy）

19.   What did you eat last night?

I _____（一條魚）

20.   Do you like to drink tea?

No, _____. I don't like it at all.

IV. 改錯

1.   I don't like drink (to drink) coffee, I like tea better.（我比較喜歡茶。）

2.   She will goes to school tomorrow.

3.   My dad didn't has a car, but he has one now.

4.   His mom can't plays the piano, she can play the guitar.

5.   What did you do next Wednesday?

6.   My teacher won't goes to Japan next week.

7.   My uncle wasn't go to America last Thursday.

8.   His daughter will reads this comic book tonight.

9.   I didn't like that movie. It is boring.

10.   He has big ear.

11.   He is tall than his brother.

12. My daughter is shorter than I am/me.

13. How much is your English books?

14. My aunt don't like to read comic books.

15. Her son can't plays soccer.

16. Was your uncle and aunt at home last night?

17. His mom weren't my teacher before.

18. I was read a comic book last night.

19. How do your mom look like?

20. Do you like drink coffee?

V. 英文該怎麼寫?

1. 我明年不會是他的老師。

   I won't be his teacher next year.

2. 他比我的弟弟矮。

   _____

3. 我比他的姊姊高。

   _____

4. 這本漫畫書比那本漫畫書重。

   _____

5. 她以前是做什麼的?(她的職業是什麼?)

   _____

6. 我的阿姨下星期五會去台北(Taipei)。

   _____

7. 他的弟弟昨晚彈了鋼琴。

   _____

8.　他以前不喜歡踢足球（play soccer）。

　　_____

9.　我的叔叔不喜歡讀英文書（English books）。

　　_____

10.　Tom 會游泳和打籃球。

　　_____

11.　她會彈吉他還是彈鋼琴？

　　_____

12.　你上個月去了哪裡？

　　_____

13.　他明天會去美國。

　　_____

14.　他們去年（last year）是你的學生嗎？

　　_____

15.　我昨天沒有洗澡。

　　_____

16.　那個女孩不喜歡玩電腦遊戲。

　　_____

17.　這件黃襯衫比那件綠襯衫好（better）。

　　_____

18.　你的手比她的手大嗎？（bigger）

　　_____

19.　John 今天下午（this afternoon）會打電話給他的媽媽嗎？

　　_____

20.　我有十個腳指趾頭。

　　_____

第十三課　過去式（肯定句）

13-5-1 填充

1.（watched）2.（ate）3.（was）4.（drank）5.（called）6.（ate）7.（played）8.（took）9.（read）10.（went）11.（was）12.（listened）13.（ate）14.（liked）15.（liked）16.（ate）17.（had）18.（had）19.（found）20.（was）21.（took）22.（played）23.（had）24.（were）25.（read）

13-5-2 改錯

1.（walks→walked）2.（find→found）3.（went→go）4.（like→liked）5.（take→took）6（find→found）7.（were→was）8.（was→were）9.（go→went）10.（is→was）11.（are→were）12.（drink→drank）13.（eat→ate）14.（call→called）15.（is→was）

13-5-3 英文怎麼寫？

1.（I watched TV last night.）2.（Your daughter called you yesterday.）3.（Their son took this book.）4.（My mom played basketball before.）5.（His dad played computer games last night.）6.（I found this book.）7.（They read that book before.）8.（It found a bird yesterday.）9.（We walked to school yesterday.）10.（They went to Japan last year.）

11.（My daughter was an engineer before.）12.（Her mom was a doctor before.）13.（I liked Coke before.）14.（He liked music before.）15.（I played basketball last week.）

第十四課　過去式 （be 動詞的否定句和問句）

14-6-1 填填看

1.（wasn't）2.（ wasn't）3.（weren't）4.（ weren't）5.（wasn't）6（wasn't）7.（wasn't）8.（weren't）9.（wasn't）10.（wasn't）11.（ wasn't）12.（wasn't）13.（wasn't）14.（weren't）15.（wasn't）

14-6-2 填填看

1.（Was was.）2.（Were weren't.）3.（ Was was.）4.（Were weren't.）5.（Was was.）

6（Was wasn't.）7.（Was was.）8.（Was wasn't.）9.（Was was.）10.（Were wasn't.）

11.（Was was.）12.（Were weren't.）13.（Was was.）14.（Was wasn't.）15.（Were weren't.）

14-6-3 英文該怎麼寫？

1.（I wasn't Ms. Lin's student before.）2.（He wasn't my teacher last year.）3.（My mom wasn't at home last week.）4.（His dad was sad yesterday.）5.（This dog wasn't big last year.）6.（I wasn't happy yesterday.）7.（My daughter wasn't happy last week.）

8.（This girl wasn't my friend last year.）9.（I wasn't at home last month.）10.（My brother wasn't an engineer last year.）

第十五課　過去式（動詞的否定句和問句）

15-6-1 填填看

1.（didn't. went）2.（didn't. played）3.（didn't. read）4.（didn't. read）5.（didn't. played）6（didn't. went）7.（didn't. liked）8.（didn't. played）9.（didn't. liked）10.（didn't like）11.（didn't drink）12.（didn't read）13.（didn't go）14.（ didn't take) 15.(didn't play)

15-6-2 問答

1.(I didn't. went) 2.(they didn't. played) 3.(she did.) 4.(she did.) 5.(he didn't. played)

6.(she did.) 7.(it didn't. drank) 8.(they didn't. went) 9.(he did.)10.(he didn't. read)

11.(it did.) 12.(I didn't. liked) 13.(I didn't. had) 14.(I did.) 15.(they did.)

15-6-3 改錯

1.(went→go) 2.(doesn't→didn't) 3.(likes→like) 4.(went→go) 5.(listened → listen) 6(played → play) 7.(don't → didn't) 8.(walks → walk) 9.(took → take) 10.(takes → take)

11.(reads→read) 12.(liked→like) 13.(likes→like) 14.(watched→watch) 15.(watched→watch)

第十六課　未來式（肯定句、否定句、問句）

16-6-2 沒有標準答案

16-6-2 填充

1.(will read) 2.(will listen) 3.(will do) 4.(will call) 5.(will go) 6(will play) 7.(will eat) 8.(will call) 9.(will watch) 10.(will eat) 11.(will play) 12.(will drink) 13.(will drink) 14.(will eat) 15.(will find)（以上皆可用won't）

16-6-3 問答

1.(I will.) 2.(I won't.) 3.(I will.) 4.(I won't.) 5.(I will.) 6(I won't.) 7. (I will.) 8.(I won't.) 9.(I will.) 10.(I won't.)11.(she will.) 12.(she won't.) 13.(he will.) 14.(it will.) 15.(I won't.)

16-6-4 英文該怎麼寫？

1.（I will go to school tomorrow.）2.（He will go to Japan next week.）3.（Will you take a shower tonight?）4.（My mom will play baseball later.）5.（My daughter will be happy next month.）6.（This doctor will read this book later.）7.（That engineer will take a nap later.）8.（This girl will call me later.）9.（Will your students come this afternoon?）

10.（They will play basketball tomorrow.）

第十七課　打招呼

17-6-1 選選看

1.（2）2.（3）3.（2）4.（2）5.（2）6（3）7.（2）8.（2）9.（3）10.（3）

17-6-2 填填看

1.（morning）2.（afternoon）3.（evening）4.（night）5.（fine）6.（later）7.（too）

8.（watches TV every day）9.（am reading a book, too）

10.（is playing computer games）11.（is an engineer）

12.（too）13.（like eggs）14.（played baseball）15.（play basketball later）

第十八課　介紹

18-6-1 填填看

1.（name is）2.（name）3.（Her）4.（Their）5.（Nice）6（from）7.（It）8.（They）9.（She）10.（from）11.（is She）12.（It）13.（It）14.（They）15.（is）

18-6-2 改錯

1.（are → is）2.（brothers' name → brother's name）3.（is → are 或 pencils → pencil）4 .（is→are）或（cakes→cake）5.（is→was）6.（meet→met）7.（are→is）或（basketball→basketballs）8.（is→are）或（brothers→brother）9.（are→ is）或（sister→sisters）10.（meet→met）

18-6-3 英文該怎麼寫？

1.（Where is his teacher from?）2.（His teacher is from America.）3.（Where is your teacher from?）4.（My teacher is from Japan.）5.（Where is their teacher from?）

6.（Their teacher is from Taiwan.）7.（My cat's name is Amy.）8.（His dog's name is John.）9.（I met Tom last year.）10.（She meets Tom every day.）

第十九課　你會嗎？

19-8-1 填填看

1.（can）2.（can't）3.（can't）4.（play can）5.（can）6（can't）7.（can is）8.（can't can）

9.（can't）10.（can't can）11.（can can）12.（can't can）13.（can't can）14.（can can）15.（can）

19-8-2 改錯

1.（walks→walk）2.（drank→drink）3.（drinks→drink）4.（swims→swim）5.（played→play）6（plays→play）7.（plays→play）8.（played→play）9.（reads→read）10.（plays→play）11.（read）12.（swims→swim）13.（met→meet）14.（listened→listen）15.（found→find）

19-8-3 英文該如何寫？

1.（I can't play the piano.）2.（My brother can't swim.）3.（Her sister can't play soccer.）

4.（Her mother can't speak English.）5.（Our father can't play the guitar.）6.（I can't meet you today.）7.（He can't go to school tomorrow.）8.（I can't drink milk now.）

9.（They can't go home now.）10.（I can't take a shower today.）

第二十課　星期幾？

20-6-1 選選看

1.(1) 2.(2) 3.(1) 4.(4) 5.(3) 6(2) 7.(2) 8.(1) 9.(1) 10.(4)

20-6-2 填填看

1.(day) 2.(Sunday)3.(Monday) 4.(Tuesday) 5.(Wednesday) 6.(Thursday) 7.(Friday) 8.(Saturday) 9.(go) 10.(weekends) 11.(plays Wednesday)12.(on) 13.(Saturday) 14.(on) 15.(ate) 16.(will) 17.(played) 18.(will) 19.(met)20.(didn't)

20-6-3 英文該怎麼寫？

1.(I watch TV at home on Sunday.) 2.(His sister goes to school on Monday.) 3.(I don't play the piano on Thursday.) 4.(I take a nap at home on Wednesday.) 5.(His dog takes a nap on Friday.) 6.(Their mom plays basketball on Saturday.) 7.(I met my doctor last Friday.) 8.(I will play soccer next Tuesday.) 9.(I will meet my teacher this Monday.)
10.(I will go to America next Saturday.)

第二十一課　　購物

21-6-1 填填看

1.(It's) 2.(It's) 3.(They're) 4.(They're) 5.(It's) 6(yellow) 7.(white) 8.(likes) 9.(likes) 10.(computer.)11.(shirt.) 12.(bird.) 13.(good book.) 14.(milk) 15.(their)

21-6-2 英文該怎麼寫？

1.(I'm looking for a small book.) 2.(My sister is looking for a good computer.) 3.(His bird is looking for water.) 4.(Our teacher is looking for a pencil.) 5.(She is looking for her mom.) 6.(This bird is looking for an egg.) 7.(Their daughter is looking for a purple bird.) 8.(I'm looking for a red shirt.)

9.（This doctor is looking for her pen.）10.（Their dog is looking for its mom.）

21-6-3 改錯

1.（is → are）2.（are → is）3.（doesn't → don't）4.（doesn't → don't）5.（do → does）6.（don't → doesn't）7.（don't → doesn't）8.（like → likes）9.（are → is）10.（watches → watch）11.（meet → met）12.（walk → walked）13.（plays → play）14.（reads → read）15.（reads → read）

第二十二課　比較

22-6-1 填填看

1.（older）2.（bigger）3.（cleaner）4.（bigger）5.（younger）6（higher）7.（better）8.（slower）9.（worse）10.（heavier）11.（older）12.（shorter）13.（taller）14.（heavier）15.（younger）16.（faster）17.（slower）18.（taller）19.（cleaner）20.（dirtier）

22-6-2 英文該怎麼寫？

1.（I'm taller than my brother.）2.（He is shorter than my brother.）3.（My mom is older than my dad.）4.（My sister is slower than I am.）5.（This cat is faster than that cat.）

6.（This book is better than that book.）7.（My brother is heavier than I am.）

8.（They are happier than we are.）9.（This bird is smaller than that bird.）

10.（This movie is longer than that movie.）11.（This desk is lighter than that chair.）

12.（Don't watch TV tonight.）13.（Don't play basketball on Monday.）

14.（Don't play the piano on Wednesday.）15.（Don't take a nap on Thursday.）

第二十三課　表示喜歡或不喜歡

23-6-1 填填看

1.（it）2.（them）3.（it）4.（it）5.（likes）6（eggs）7.（likes）8.（it）9.（them）10.（it）
11.（like）12.（cute）13.（boring）14.（it）15.（he）16.（they）17.（all）18.（they）
19.（at）20.（it）

23-6-2 改錯

1.（like watch→like to watch）2.（like→likes）3.（likes read→likes to read）4.
（do → doesn't）5.（likes play → likes to play）6（it → them）7.（he → him）8.
（like go→ like to go）9.（don't→ doesn't）10.（don't→ doesn't）11.（like go→
like to go）12.（don't → doesn't）13.（like watch → like to watch）14.（don't →
doesn't）15.（like play→like to play）

23-6-3 用英文怎麼寫？

1.（I like to take a shower every day.）2.（He doesn't like to watch TV at all.）3.
（This English book is boring.）4.（My mom doesn't like to eat fish.）5.（My
brother doesn't like to eat fish, either.）6.（Does he like to play baseball?）7.
（My teacher likes to play the guitar very much.）8.（She doesn't like to drink
milk.）9.（My dad doesn't like purple shirts.）10.（Her daughter doesn't like black
bags.）

第二十四課　形容長相

24-6-1 填填看

1.（short）2.（small）3.（bigger）4.（longer）5.（legs）6（eyes）7.（short）8.（head）
9.（nose）10.（ears）11.（legs）12.（mouth）13.（shoulder）14.（head）15.（bag）
16.（are）17.（is）18.（is）19.（are）20.（are）

24-6-2 英文該怎麼寫？

1.（ Look, that monster has two heads!）2.（Look, this monster has five hands!）

3.（Look, this monster has seven mouths!）4.（Look, this dog has five legs.）5.（Look, this cat has three ears.）6.（Where is your nose?）7.（Where are your hands?）8.（Where are your ears?）9.（Where are your toes?）10.（Where are your shoulders?）

I . 選擇題

1.(1) 2.(3) 3.(2) 4.(3) 5.(2) 6(1) 7.(3) 8.(1) 9.(3) 10.(2) 11.(1) 12.(3) 13.(2) 14.(1) 15.(3) 16(1) 17.(2) 18.(3) 19.(3) 20.(1)

II . 填充題

1. can't 2. won't 3. engineer 4. either 5. is 6. didn't 7.didn't 8. Will或Can 9. ate 10. older 11. can't或won't 12.Were 13.Did 14.Will 15. names 16. listen 17.found 18.worse 19.on 20.from

III . 問答

1. He's from Nantou. 2. I can. 3.a purple shirt. 4.I didn't. 5.I was. 6.a teacher. 7.called her friend. 8.she didn't. 9.listened to music. 10.will do his homework later. 11.she will. 12. dog. 13.brown. 14.will play the piano. 15.It's boring. 16. one hundred NT dollars. 17.am looking for a clean shirt. 18.name is Amy. 19. ate a fish. 20.I don't.

IV . 改錯

1. drink→to drink 2.goes→go 3.has→have 4.plays→play 5.did→will 6. goes→go 7.wasn't→didn't 8.reads→read 9. is→was 10.ear→ears 11.

tall→taller 12.short→shorter 13.is→are 14.don't→doesn't 15.plays→play 16. Was → Were 17.weren't → wasn't 18.去 was 19.do → does 20.drink → to drink

Ⅴ.英文該怎麼寫？

1.I won't be his teacher next year. 2.He is shorter than my brother. 3.I'm taller than his sister. 4. This comic book is heavier than that one（comic book）. 5. What did she do before? 6. My aunt will go to Taipei next Friday. 7.His brother played the piano last night. 8.He didn't like to play soccer before. 9.My uncle doesn't like to read English books. 10.Tom can swim and play basketball. 11. Can she play the guitar or piano? 12.Where did you go last month? 13.He will go to America tomorrow. 14.Were they your students last year? 15.I didn't take a shower yesterday. 16.That girl doesn't like to play computer games. 17.This yellow shirt is better than that green shirt. 18.Are your hands bigger than her hands? 19.Will John call his mom this afternoon? 20.I have ten toes.

專門替中國人寫的英文課本 *初級本（下冊）*

2003年9月初版　　　　　　　　　　　　　定價：新臺幣170元
2006年10月初版第十二刷
2007年1月二版
2010年2月二版八刷
有著作權・翻印必究
Printed in Taiwan.

著　　　　者	文	庭	澍	
策 劃 審 訂	李	家	同	
發 行 人	林	載	爵	

出　　版　　者 聯 經 出 版 事 業 股 份 有 限 公 司	責 任 編 輯	何 采 嬪
地　　　　址 台 北 市 忠 孝 東 路 四 段 5 5 5 號	校　　　對	楊 蕙 苓
總　經　銷 聯 合 發 行 股 份 有 限 公 司	整 體 設 計	陳 玉 嵐
發　行　所:台北縣新店市寶橋路235巷6弄6號2F		
電話：(0 2) 2 9 1 7 8 0 2 2		
台北忠孝門市：台北市忠孝東路四段561號1F		
電話：(0 2) 2 7 6 8 3 7 0 8		
台北新生門市：台 北 市 新 生 南 路 三 段 9 4 號		
電話：(0 2) 2 3 6 2 0 3 0 8		
台中分公司：台 中 市 健 行 路 3 2 1 號		
暨 門 市 電 話：(0 4) 2 2 3 7 1 2 3 4 ext.5		
高雄辦事處：高 雄 市 成 功 一 路 3 6 3 號 2F		
電話：(0 7) 2 2 1 1 2 3 4 ext.5		
郵 政 劃 撥 帳 戶 第 0 1 0 0 5 5 9 - 3 號		
郵 撥 電 話： 2 7 6 8 3 7 0 8		
印 刷 者 世 和 印 製 企 業 有 限 公 司		

行政院新聞局出版事業登記證局版臺業字第0130號

國家圖書館出版品預行編目資料

專門替中國人寫的英文課本　初級本
（下冊）／文庭澍著．李家同策劃．審訂．
二版．臺北市：聯經，2007 年（民 96）
120 面；19×26 公分．
ISBN　978-957-08-3125-2(平裝附光碟片)
〔2010年2月二版八刷〕
1.英國語言　–讀本

805.18　　　　　　　　　　　96001517